READ with me! *has been written using about 800 words and these include the 300 Key Words.*

In the first six books, all words introduced occur again in the following book to provide vital repetition in the early stages. The number of new words increases as the child gains confidence and progresses through the stories.

After Book 6, a wider range of vocabulary is used but each word is repeated at least three times within that story.

The stories centre on the everyday lives of Kate, Tom, Sam the dog, Mum, Dad, friends, neighbours and relations. This setting often provides a springboard into Tom and Kate's world of make-believe. Also, the humorous, colourful illustrations include picture story sequences to stimulate the reader's own language and imagination.

A complete list of stories is given on the back cover and suggestions for using each book are made on the back pages.

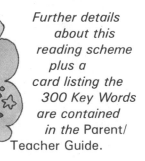

Further details about this reading scheme plus a card listing the 300 Key Words are contained in the Parent/Teacher Guide.

This book belongs to

_____

_____

British Library Cataloguing in Publication Data
Murray, W. (William), *(date)*
    The big secret.
    1. English language—Readers
    I. Title   II. Corby, Jill   III. Hines, Marida   IV. Series
    428.6
    ISBN 0-7214-1324-2

First edition

Published by Ladybird Books Ltd Loughborough Leicestershire UK
Ladybird Books Inc Auburn Maine 04210 USA

© LADYBIRD BOOKS LTD MCMXC
*All rights reserved. No part of this publication may be reproduced, stored in a retrieval
system, or transmitted in any form or by any means, electronic, mechanical, photo-copying,
recording or otherwise, without the prior consent of the copyright owner.*

Printed in England (3)

READ with me!

The big secret

by WILLIAM MURRAY
stories by JILL CORBY
illustrated by MARIDA HINES

Ladybird Books

Dad asks them to sit down and have something to eat.

"What would you like, Tom?" his mother asks. "Will you have some of this?"

"Kate, what would you like? Some of this as well?"

"I've got some days off now," says Dad to Tom and Kate. "So I'll look after you. Mum, you can go and get ready for work."

"I think we shall look after you,
Dad," Tom tells him.

Mum goes to get ready.

"Do you think Mum will like her
work?" asks Kate.

"She will have to see," Dad tells her,
"but I think she will like it."

Mum comes down.
"I'm ready. I'll go
now," she says.
"Goodbye, Kate.
Eat up. Goodbye
Tom. Be a good
boy. I'm off now.
Goodbye."

"Now listen, you two," says Dad.
"It's Mum's birthday on Saturday so
we must think of something to give
her."

"She has got lots and lots of things,"
says Tom. "What can we think of
that's new for her?"

"We shall have to go to the shops
and look for a present," Kate tells
them.

"Yes," says Dad. "But before we go,
we must think of what we would like
to get."

"I think that she would like some
flowers," Tom tells him. "Can I get
some flowers for her present, Dad?"

"Yes," Dad says. "You can get some flowers."

"She will have to have something to put the flowers in," says Kate. "I'll get a new vase," she says. "Yes, that's it, a new vase."

Then they get ready to go to the shops to buy the presents for their mother's birthday on Saturday.

"Come on," says Dad, "we'll get into the car now and go and buy the presents."

"I know Mum's name," says Kate. "It's Jenny."

"Yes," says Dad. "Her name is Jenny."

"Now," says Dad, "I think we'll buy the vase but we won't get the flowers before Saturday."

"Why not?" they ask. "Why can't we get them now?"

Dad tells them that if they buy the flowers now, they won't last. "That's why," he says.

"We must get them on Saturday for them to last," he tells them. "But we'll look at the flowers now, to see which ones you would like to give to Mum."

"Here we are," he says. "I'll put the car here."

They go into the flower shop.

"There are lots of vases over there," Kate tells Dad. "I'll have a look."

Tom goes to look at the flowers.

"Dad, I like all these flowers," he says.

"Which ones do you like best?" asks his father.

"I think that I like those yellow ones best of all," says Tom.

"Yes," Dad says. "I think those will last well and be just right for your mum."

Tom tells the girl in the shop which flowers he would like to buy.

Then Dad says, "But we won't take them now. We want them on Saturday, please."

"Can I have your name, please?"
asks the girl. "Then I'll take them to
your home on Saturday."

"I know which vase I would like for
Mum," Kate tells her dad. "I like that
blue one."

"Right," says Dad. "I'll get the blue
vase down for you."

11

"Tom knows which flowers he wants to buy, and Kate has got the vase," Dad says. "So now I must buy a present for Mum."

They stop to look at a shop.

"I think she would like a ring. So we'll go in here and look at some," Dad tells them.

"There are lots of rings here," says Kate.

"Which ring would Mum like best?"
asks Dad. "Do you think she would
like this blue one or that red one, or
this yellow one, or those over there?"

"She would like that one best, Dad,"
Tom tells him.

"Yes, why not!" Dad says. "That
one does look about right. I'm going
to have it. I'll have that ring please,"
he says to the girl.

"Right," says Dad. "Now that's
done, we can go home."

As they are going home in the car,
Dad tells them that now they must
think about a party.

"We are going to have a party for
Mum, a surprise party," he says.

"Who shall we ask to the party?"
asks Kate.

"We shall ask all Mum's best
friends," Dad tells them. "It's Mum's
party, so we shall ask her friends."

"There will be many things to get ready, so you two will have to help me," he tells them.

"Yes," Tom says. "We will have to make lots of things to eat, as so many friends will be coming."

"Here we are, at home. Do you think that Mum has got home before us?" Dad asks them. "If she has, these presents will have to stay in the car so she won't see them."

Their father tells them that they must think who they would like to ask to the party. He writes down the names of all Mum's friends.

''Now we can write all the invitations,'' he tells them.

Tom and Kate help Dad to write the invitations and write all the names on them.

"If this is a surprise party," says Tom, "it will have to be a secret."

"That's right," Kate says. "Mum must not know about it."

"We shall put **This is a big secret** on the invitations, then everyone will know that they must not tell Mum," Tom tells them. They write it on all the invitations.

"Can you two keep a big secret like this?" Dad asks.

DO YOU THINK THEY CAN KEEP THE SECRET?

"The presents can't stay here," says Dad.

"No," Tom says. "Or Mum will see them when she comes home from work."

"So we shall have to hide them," says Kate. "Where shall we hide them?"

"In here, or in there?" Tom asks. "Mum doesn't look in here much."

They hide the presents just as Mum comes in from work.

18

"How are you?" she asks Dad.
"How are you two? What have you
done all day?"

"Not a lot," Tom tells her.

But Kate says, "It's a big secret and
we can't tell you."

"Stop it, Kate," Tom says. "Don't
say that."

Mum asks, "What can it be?"

When their mother next goes to work,
they get some more things ready for
her birthday party.

The next day, when their mother has gone to work, they make her birthday cards.

"She must have cards for her birthday," Tom says.

"That's right," says Dad.

"I'll get the paints," says Kate.

"And I'll look for some card," says Tom. "I think there will be some in here, or is it in there?"

They paint the cards. Tom paints a
dragon like the one by his bed. Kate
paints Sam with his rabbit. She
knows that her mother likes Sam very
much, and that Sam likes his rabbit.
She thinks they will look good on her
birthday card.

They show their cards to their father.

"Fantastic," he says. "Your cards
are fantastic!"

Kate shows her card to Sam. He
looks at it and goes to get his rabbit.
He looks just the same as the card.

The next day, Mum gets ready for work. They all say goodbye to her. As soon as she has gone, they get everything ready to make the cake.

"We shall have to make a very big cake as so many friends are coming," Tom tells them.

"Yes," says Dad. "It will have to be big. I think this will do."

"How many candles shall we have on the cake?" Kate asks. "We have lots of candles. Some are red, some are yellow and some are blue."

"How many candles have we got? asks Tom.

"We shall just put all the candles on," Dad tells them. "I think that will do."

"Kate, take this, please," Dad tells her. "And Tom, can you put this down, please. Now, have we got everything here?"

Everything is ready for the cake, so now they can make it. Dad lets Kate do the mixing. Then Tom has a turn. He can do the mixing as well.

"Two of these go in now," says Dad, "and some of that next. It all has to go into the cake.

"Let me have a turn at mixing," he says. "Mixing soon makes you tired. Let me have a go when you two get tired.

"I think that will do now," Dad tells them. "The cake is ready now. We can put it in here."

"That looks fantastic, Dad," Tom says. "It's just as good as the ones Mum makes."

"But Mum's cakes are not as big as this," Kate tells him.

"Next, we must make the cake look very fancy," says Tom. "It will be a fantastic surprise for Mum on Saturday."

"I think that she will like it very much," Dad tells them.

"Let me paint a blue vase, please. Just like the one that I got from the shop," says Kate.

Tom paints yellow flowers just like the ones in the shop.

Next, they have to write 'Happy Birthday Mum' on the cake. Dad lets Tom write it.

"How do I do it, Dad?" he asks.

"I'll show you how to do it," Dad says.

Now they must hide the cake, so that Mum does not see it before Saturday. Where can they hide it?

"I think it can go in here," Dad tells them. "Mum does not look in here much."

When their mother comes home from work, she does not know what Tom and Kate have done. But she does know that they have a big secret. Kate said so. So she looks round to see if there is anything strange anywhere. But she can't see anything strange anywhere.

So she goes to get something for them to eat. She lets Tom help her to get things ready.

"You are a big help to me," she tells Tom. "I have done so much work that I'm tired."

"Do you like your work?" Tom asks.

"Yes, I like it a lot," says his mother. "Yes, Dad said you would like it. He said you would like it very much," says Tom.

When Saturday comes, Dad tells Tom and Kate to take Sam for a walk.

He tells them that their mother must go with them so that he can get everything ready for the surprise party. And he says that they must not let her come home before 4 o'clock.

By 4 o'clock all the friends who have had invitations will have come and everything will be ready. Then they can come home from the walk.

So Kate and Tom go to tell Mum that it is time for Sam's walk.

"You have to come with us," they say. "Dad can't come."

They get ready and off they go.

"We shall be home soon," Mum tells Dad.

"No we won't," Tom tells Kate. "Not before 4 o'clock."

They walk a long way. Sam likes the long walk. He likes to run about and jump up with Kate and Tom.

Mum says, "It's time to go home now."

"No," says Tom. "We must go over there first."

They walk on and on. Kate is tired but she will not say anything.

"We shall have to go home now," says Mum.

Tom looks at a clock. It is not time to go home.

"Can we just go to the library?" Tom asks.

"What do you want to go to the library for?" asks his mother.

"I must get some books on dragons for school," he tells her.

"All right," says Mum. "We will go to the library. But Sam will have to stay outside."

As they go into the library, they look at the clock. "It's not 4 o'clock for a long time," Tom tells Kate. "I shall have to take a long time in here."

At first he can't see anything anywhere about dragons. Then he sees some dragon books. There are not many of them. He looks at them to see which he likes best. He takes a long time.

"Come on, Tom. You must come now," says his mother. "Dad won't know where we are."

"Shall I take these two or those two?"
Tom asks her. "Which do you think?"

Mum looks at the books. Tom looks
at the clock. It will soon be 4 o'clock.
Tom talks to his mother about the
books. Then he sees that the clock
says 4 o'clock.

"Right," he tells her. "I'll have these
two and we'll go home."

"At long last," says Mum.

They all get home at last.

"You must have had a very long walk," Dad says.

Mum goes in to sit down. Then comes the surprise!

Everyone jumps out and sings,
> *Happy birthday to you;*
> *Happy birthday to you.*
> *Happy birthday dear Jenny.*
> *Happy birthday to you.*

"That's our mum's name – Jenny," Tom tells Kate.

"I know Mum's name is Jenny," she says.

Mum is very surprised and very pleased to see everyone. Kate gives her mum the vase. Mum likes it and she says thank you very much.

Tom asks his dad where the flowers are. He can't see them anywhere. Then he sees them coming and runs outside to get them. He gives them to his mother. She puts some water in the vase and then she puts in the flowers. She says thank you and looks very happy.

Everyone gives Mum presents. Dad gives her the ring. But little Lucy, Kate's friend, can't get to Mum to give her a present. Kate helps her to get to her mother.

"How are you, Lucy? What's this?" asks Mum. "This is a fantastic present. Thank you very much."

Then Kate and Tom show their mum all the things they have made. "Have you made all this?" she asks.

"Come and eat, everyone," they shout. And then they show their mum the cake.

"We made it with Dad," they tell her.

"What a surprise, and so many candles," she says.

They all eat a lot and they all talk a lot. Then Kate sings and Tom sings. They sing, *Happy birthday dear Mum.*

Everyone is happy.

Just look at Lucy. She has some cake.

Mum puts on some of her presents.
She looks very happy.

Then all their friends say goodbye.
They say that they have had a very
happy time and they say thank you to
Tom and Kate and their dad. Lucy
comes to say thank you as well. They
all say goodbye and go home.

"That was the best party that I've had," Mum tells them. "Thank you all, my dears, very much. I had a very happy time with all my friends. You said you had a big secret, Kate. Now I know, don't I?

"You two can keep a secret very well," she tells them.

"And it was a very big secret," Kate and Tom say.

Words introduced in this book

Number of words.....................................63

Where are Tom, Kate and Mum?

What is the book about?

What time is it?

Notes for using this book

The words, pictures and planning of this book are designed to:

* help the child to learn to read
* help you to make learning an exciting and enjoyable experience for her*
* encourage lots of conversation
* help her to become confident in her own ability
* encourage her powers of observation, understanding and sense of humour.

When your child is ready and keen to learn to read (a Reading Readiness checklist is given in the Parent/Teacher Guide) introduce this book just like any other picture storybook. Find a quiet, comfortable place and either read the book all the way through or read and talk about one page at a time. Point to the words and show that reading goes from left to right.

* To avoid the clumsy he/she, him/her, we have referred to the child as "she".
All the books are of course equally suited to both boys and girls.